Thomas
Breaks a Promise

Illustrated by Richard Courtney

A GOLDEN BOOK · NEW YORK

Thomas the Tank Engine & Friends®

A BRITT ALLCROFT COMPANY PRODUCTION

Based on The Railway Series by The Reverend W Awdry   Copyright © 2006 Gullane (Thomas) LLC
Thomas the Tank Engine & Friends and Thomas & Friends are trademarks of Gullane Entertainment, Inc.
Thomas the Tank Engine & Friends is Reg. U.S. Pat. TM Off.

A HIT Entertainment Company

Library of Congress Control Number: 2005932249
ISBN: 0-375-83671-3
www.randomhouse.com/kids/thomas
www.goldenbooks.com
www.thomasandfriends.com
PRINTED IN THE UNITED STATES OF AMERICA
First Golden Books Edition 2006   10 9 8

The seasons were changing on the Island of Sodor. The leaves had begun to change color, and the air was growing crisp. Thomas the Tank Engine was feeling restless.

"Summer is almost over, and I haven't had any real fun," he complained.

"You're a fussy little engine," replied Gordon. "We're not here to have fun. We're here to work."

Well, that didn't make Thomas feel any better.

"I'd rather be fussy and fun than bossy and boring!" he retorted.

The next morning, Sir Topham Hatt called the engines together.

"We're opening a new branch line tomorrow," he told them. "I need one of you to check the signals on the new line to see that they're all working properly. Who will volunteer?"

"I will," Thomas piped up. "I promise to check very carefully." Checking signals wasn't much fun, but it was better than being bossed around in the train yard.

"Off you go, then," said Sir Topham Hatt. "And be sure to check every signal, Thomas. Safety is our first concern."

Something about shiny new tracks always put Thomas in a good mood. He whistled merrily as he rolled along the new branch line. "Checking signals is really useful," he thought. "Safety is our first concern."

Each time he saw a signal, Thomas made sure that the arm was in the right position. He also checked to see that the signal lamp was working, so it could be seen at night.

If the signal arm was down and the lamp was red,
that meant danger on the tracks ahead.
There were hidden junctions . . .

... hanging rocks ...

... dangerous curves ...

. . . and steep hills.

Thomas had almost reached the end of the new branch line when he saw the sign for a carnival. There was nothing Thomas loved more than a carnival. Oh, how he would love to go!

"If I hurry to the carnival now, I can check the rest of the signals later," he told himself. And with that, Thomas turned off and headed into the countryside.

Carnival
TODAY ONLY!

The carnival was splendid. There were games and rides and cotton candy. And there were lots of children.

"Look, it's Thomas!" they cried, and ran to greet their favorite blue engine.

When Thomas got back to the train yard, Sir Topham Hatt was waiting.

"You've been gone a long time, Thomas," he said. "You must have done a very thorough job of checking the signals on the new branch line."

"Yes, sir," peeped Thomas. But suddenly he realized that he'd forgotten to go back and finish the job. He had broken his promise! But how could he tell that to Sir Topham Hatt?

"Good." Sir Topham Hatt beamed. "Then everything is ready for tomorrow's grand opening."

Thomas gulped. What if there was trouble? What if one of the unchecked signals didn't work?

"I know," thought Thomas. "I'll get up very early tomorrow and go out to check the rest of the signals before the grand opening."

That night, Percy was being loaded for his mail run when a call came into the station. Rain had washed out a section of track on the mail route. Percy would have to find a way around.

"Don't worry, Percy." Sir Topham Hatt smiled. "You can take the new branch line."

Off Percy went, pulling two big cars loaded with mail.

The rain fell heavily. Each time Percy saw a red signal lamp, he slowed carefully until he had passed the dangerous spot. Then suddenly, in the dark, Percy passed another signal. The lamp was not lit, so he didn't see it until too late. The arm was down, for danger! Percy slammed on his brakes, but the rain made the tracks slippery. And there it was ahead—a *very* dangerous curve.

"Oh, no!" cried Percy. He closed his eyes and did his best to hold on through the turn.

CRASH! One of the mail cars flew off the tracks and was smashed to bits. Percy shivered with fear from his close call.

The next morning, Thomas awoke and sneaked out of his shed. Then he saw Percy returning with Sir Topham Hatt.

"Percy has had a terrible fright," Sir Topham said sternly. "He almost derailed because of a signal lamp that didn't work. How could such a thing have happened, Thomas?"

"Oh, sir! I'm so sorry, sir," Thomas sputtered. And it all came rushing out—about the carnival, and the children, and about how he'd forgotten to go back and finish the job.

"I'm sorry I broke my promise, sir," said Thomas sheepishly. "I just wanted to be part of the fun, and then I forgot."

"There will be no fun for you for quite some time," Sir Topham Hatt scolded. "Percy will run your branch line until you've gone and checked every signal on my railway—twice!"

And now, every time Thomas passes a signal, he checks it twice, just to be safe.

Gordon likes to tease him. "Fussy little Thomas certainly is fussy about signals."

"Peep, peep!" says Thomas. "Safety is our first concern."